SUPER FAITH

Spi-net Girl

Web of Wisdom

Miss Donna Ricketts

author**HOUSE**®

AuthorHouse™ UK
1663 Liberty Drive
Bloomington, IN 47403 USA
www.authorhouse.co.uk
Phone: UK TFN: 0800 0148641 (Toll Free inside the UK)
*   UK Local: (02) 0369 56322 (+44 20 3695 6322 from outside the UK)*

Published by AuthorHouse   02/14/2023

ISBN: 979-8-8230-8083-5 (sc)
ISBN: 979-8-8230-8084-2 (e)

Library of Congress Control Number: 2023902426

Print information available on the last page.

Contents

Acknowledgements

This book is written in honour, of my late perents; Mr & Mrs Ricketts. May they continue to enjoy heaven every day eternally, because they were worriors of the faith, and every thought, fourt for their children, raised their family team, and I must say they finished well, Allelujah Yeshua!

From Sister to Sister!

Please let me encourage you, by the LORD's grace, I just wanted to say that you are GOD's special daughter and HE loves you, so much- and so do I.

I hope you like your shoes of peace, helmet of salvation, breastplate of righteousness, girdle of truth. . . and the rest follow, from the book of Ephesians, and remember; aim higher!. . . .Skies the LORD.

Forever Sisters!

Trials of Life

The trials of life make you.

The trials of life break you.

The trials of life scare you.

The trials of life dare you.

Through the trials love comes through

Through the trials love can be broken too.

Life without trials, we couldn't be content.

Life without trials, we wouldn't know our strength,

Is heaven sent.

Our FATHER in heaven knows how, and knows it best!

Be blessed, forevermore.

Let Me Tell You, Words Of Wisdom (The List)

1. Be trust worthy - If you are allowed to work, in an area without a teacher, show that you are able to do it properly. Leave the area tidy and ready for use, by the next group.

2. Use Equipment Responsibly – If you use musical instruments, art equipment etc, for your work, take care and report any damage.

3. Do your homework!! – You can't hope to get a grading from the LORD, without putting in extra time outside of lessons.

4. Take responsibility in your own learning – This spiritual course is about *your* ideas and responses. It can not be *taught*, by a teacher and is not about learning facts!

5. Ask for help – This is a difficult course to do, very well in. A and B grades are not handed out, without quite deep understanding and good book research. It is worth asking your teacher, (who ever they may be), which had many years of experience, in teaching the course. Talking about your ideas, will help to guide you down the right and correct path.

6. Take advice! – If your teacher suggests a way of tackling a problem, go with it. Your teacher will know where the marks are! *May I add, GOD himself.*

7. Use your time wisely – Many pupils find that, despite thinking they have got ages to finish their project, they run out of time. Have a time-plan, (you'll also get marks, from the LORD. Manage your time. Excuses when it is too late, will be useless!

Spi-net Girl became who she was in
Christ power of the Holy Ghost

Spi-net was followed by God, for a long time and he picked her up, to be apart of his salvation kingdom, (as been rescued from hell and distruction.

At first, she used to be a horrible little sinner, felt isolated, had a lack of friend, an angry youth, not having much.

Life at home with her parents was tough, because they didn't have much. Miraculously God provided but Spi-net, she had to work hard for it! (lol)!

On one special day, her sister Samantha invited her to a gospel concert. In busy atmosphere, where a mighty man named RP, invited Spi-net to Yeshua, she surrendered her will over to the Lord.

Spi-net Words of Comfort

Choosing to love with respect not based on feelings

Offering to help in times of need

Having a listening ear

Showing genuine concern when someone is struggling

Being willing to pray for person in need

Sewing Protection Walls - GOD's Idea

Message from Spi-net- Bist. . . . GOD's protection is always fined in obscurity

And sorry, not everyone has your back, one thing I find is when GOD will give you the tools

Such as the defence wall or protection, respect, self-awareness, dignity and so forth.

Never allow negativity stop you living GOD's dream, this is waiting for you.

I like to offer you a piece of advise grab and glean, safety, logic, care for your self worth.

Good news, once you receive the LORD of his shield,

When Early Wisdom Became Her Ally

Some times you are faced with situations, where you are left to respond rationally. Take time and ease of pressure, give yourself space and make sure your mind is clear first, before you do anything.

Consult the Father and spend time with Him. Talk to the LORD and search the holy scriptures to find guidance.

Wisdom is a great friend that offers relentless assistance, never feel ashamed or embarrassed to ask.

A word of advice; look, listen and be observant at all times. (From a clear older and wise woman.

When for example, check yourself and show that you care, do not take people for advantage.

As life goes on, you will need a helping hand and you can offer help as well.

The Busy Fool

I was out at fellowship, last night, dropped into bed. . . . .but I didn't pray!

I woke up the next morning, rushing for work, "my goodness, it's 8:30. . . . . . .!"

"Sorry LORD, what did you say?"

Too busy dealing with my life, too busy in church, doing the LORD's work.

I feel week, my self inflicted trials hurt, "ouch! My fault." "LORD, where are you!?"

HE's watching, patiently HE waits, longing to have communion with you.#

"Dear LORD, Where have I been? I'm so sorry."

I must spend time with my FATHER in heaven, longing to hear from HIM again.

"GOD, what do you require from me? For your servant is listening."

I must pick up my bible and read it, for GOD has a lot to say. "Teach me your will, show me your way. . . . ." Before I start each day, I must listen, I must pray, I need HIS mercy, I need his GRACE.

For one day, I will behold HIS face. But in order to, I must seek my MASTER daily, that is what HE requires of me. . . . . . .Amen

Who Is Like The LORD!

Reach for the cross,

Don't let life or troubles hold you back.

Reach for the cross,

I said don't let it hold you back.

Again, reach for the cross,

It's up to you.

It's your decision.

But I say, choose CHRIST for life, and be covered by HIS protection.

Tender Mercy

I can't believe that someone would still care for me, when I didn't.

I actually believed that I was living for a hopeless purpose, and yet I get Confused.

If there's one thing that I have forgotten, that is I am sinful and I will never be perfect .But still there is a reason for believing, because JESUS still and always love me, regardless of my faults. . . . . . .But I also need to recognize, where and what HE has taken me from. Full stop.

I Apologize

I apologize for taking advantage of my life. I apologize for blaspheming the LORD JESUS CHRIST. I'm sorry for treating the bible with contempt, forgive me am sorry, please except my apology.

How can you love me, when I hated you? Your love is sure, it is so true. My life has been a lie, running from GOD, filled with pride, I duck, I hide. Many nights I cried, every time, I try. Many occasions, I asked "Why?". For a long time, I have put up a fight. Questioning, challenging THE MOST HIGH. LORD, I apologize. Excuses do not change my plight, without CHRIST. Trying to be, with all of my might.

GOD, I except, you are right, I apologize.

If you are willing to forgive, then I am willing to trust, I'm sorry for causing much fuss.

My ego has gone bust, for I am nothing but dust. GOD I have had enough. This life is tough, I Know I must, be cleansed by your blood. Cover me, with your love, I know I am wrong and you Have (and always will be) right. Let me live pleasing to your sight, I want to be close to you so tight. LORD I apologize. Amen

My Friend

I cry to JESUS, because I need HIM, for HE is my best friend and tell HIM, any thing.

I need HIS touch and presence, to restore me.

JESUS, I love the person and name.

I know that HE is listing to my every prayer, each day.

My life belongs to HIM totally.

I love you LORD, please keep me in you.

Spiritual Revision......Passing Life's Test

When you come to know your FATHER, be aware! You will be tested, whether small or great, long or short, be prepared. No need to be scared, just revise. Read the bible and learn, you a disciple after all, think "GOD wants to certify me, when I reach heaven". So study hard but only with GOD, as your tutor, you do need HIS help. . . . .Huuuum, the test of patience, study the gospel books of JESUS, remember how he learned. Follow HIS example.. . .What's the result? Have you failed? Don't worry, keep trying. . . .the test of courtesy. . . .forgiveness .... Love. . . .pride. . . .selfishness . Your adversary, the devil, is a cheater, a liar, selling to discourage you, don't follow his books, because they are not genuine. You will fail, if you follow him.

The great cloud of witnesses are waiting to have a ceremony for you, to be awarded by JESUS CHRIST the EXAMINER. HIS mark is all that matters! Amen

About the Author

Miss D Ricketts likes to be a positive influence, and encourage people all around her. Filled with life and joy, just to know that YESHUA, HOLY GHOST, THE GOD Head, is her savior and LORD over all her circumstances. She has learnt to overcome many challenges, and continues to strive for integrity and excellence every single day! What keeps her going is to know that she has a loving family, and good friends network and granted with helps, to her benefit.

If you would like to get in touch with her, please send emails to her- blacbeuty@ gmail.com

Printed in the United States
by Baker & Taylor Publisher Services